Goldilocks and the Three Bears

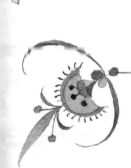

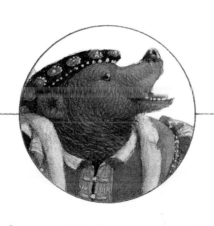

Retold
and
illustrated by

Gennady Spirin

Goldilocks and the Three Bears

MARSHALL CAVENDISH CHILDREN

Marshall Cavendish Corporation, 99 White Plains Road, Tarrytown, NY 10591

www.marshallcavendish.us/kids

LIBRARY OF CONGRESS CATALOGING-IN-PUBLICATION DATA

Spirin, Gennady. Goldilocks and the three bears / retold and illustrated by Gennady

Spirin. — 1st ed. p. cm. Summary: A simplified retelling of the adventures of a little

girl walking in the woods who finds the house of the three bears and helps herself to

their belongings. Includes a note on the history of the tale. ISBN 978-0-7614-5596-7

[1. Folklore. 2. Bears—Folklore.] I. Goldilocks and the three bears English. II. Title.

PZ8.1.S76733Gol 2009 398.2—dc22 [E] 2008026984

The illustrations are rendered in watercolor and colored pencil.

Book design by Michael Nelson   Editor: Margery Cuyler

Printed in China First edition

1 3 5 6 4 2

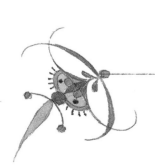 Marshall Cavendish
Children

For Lydia Stepanoff

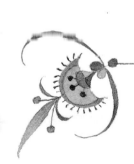

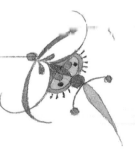

Once upon a time,
there were three bears—
a papa bear, a mama bear,
and a little baby bear.

Every morning they ate porridge for breakfast.
Papa Bear had a great big bowl.

Mama Bear had a middle-sized bowl.
And Little Bear had a tiny little bowl just right for him.

After breakfast, they sat in their three special chairs.
Papa Bear had a great big chair.
Mama Bear had a middle-sized chair.
And Little Bear had a tiny little chair just right for him.

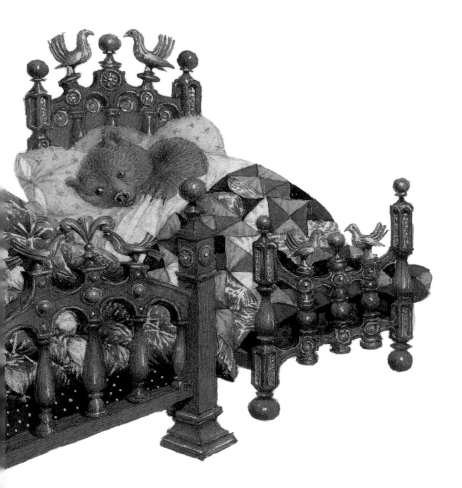

At night the bears slept in their three special beds.
Papa Bear had a great big bed.
Mama Bear had a middle-sized bed.
And Little Bear had a tiny little bed just right for him.

One morning Papa Bear said, "This porridge
is *waaaaaay* too hot."
"Yes, it is," said Mama Bear.
"Yes, it is," said Little Bear.
So the three bears took a walk while it
cooled off.
After they left, a little girl named
Goldilocks peeked in the window.
"Mmmm," she said, "that porridge smells
very good and I'm *very* hungry."
So she climbed inside.

First she tasted the porridge in the great big bowl.
"Too hot!" she said.

Then she tasted the porridge in the middle-sized bowl.
"Too cold!" she said.

Finally she tasted the porridge in the tiny little bowl.

It was neither too hot nor too cold.

It was just right!

Goldilocks ate it all up.

Then she tried sitting in the three chairs.
First she sat in the great big chair.
"Too hard!" she said.

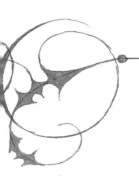

Then she sat in the middle-sized chair.

"Too soft!" she said.

Finally she sat in the tiny little chair.

It was neither too hard nor too soft.

It was just right!

But all of a sudden, the little chair broke!

Goldilocks landed on the floor.

"That hurt," she said. "I need to lie down."

Soon, the three bears came home.

"Who's been eating my porridge?" said Papa Bear.

"Who's been eating *my* porridge?" said Mama Bear.

"My porridge is all gone!" said Little Bear.

First she lay on the great big bed.

"Too hard!" she said.

Then she lay on the middle-sized bed.

"Too soft!" she said.

Finally she lay on the tiny little bed.

It was neither too hard nor too soft.

It was just right!

Goldilocks fell fast asleep.

"Who's been sitting in my chair?" said Papa Bear.
"Who's been sitting in *my* chair?" said Mama Bear.
"My chair's broken!" said Little Bear.

"Who's been sleeping in my bed?"
   said Papa Bear.
"Who's been sleeping in *my* bed?"
   said Mama Bear.
"Look, there's someone in my bed!"
   said Little Bear. "And there she is!"

Goldilocks woke up and saw the three bears.
She leaped up and ran out of the house.
"Bye," said Papa Bear in his great big voice.
"Bye," said Mama Bear in her middle-sized voice.
"Bye," said Little Bear in his tiny little voice.

And that's the
end of the
story!

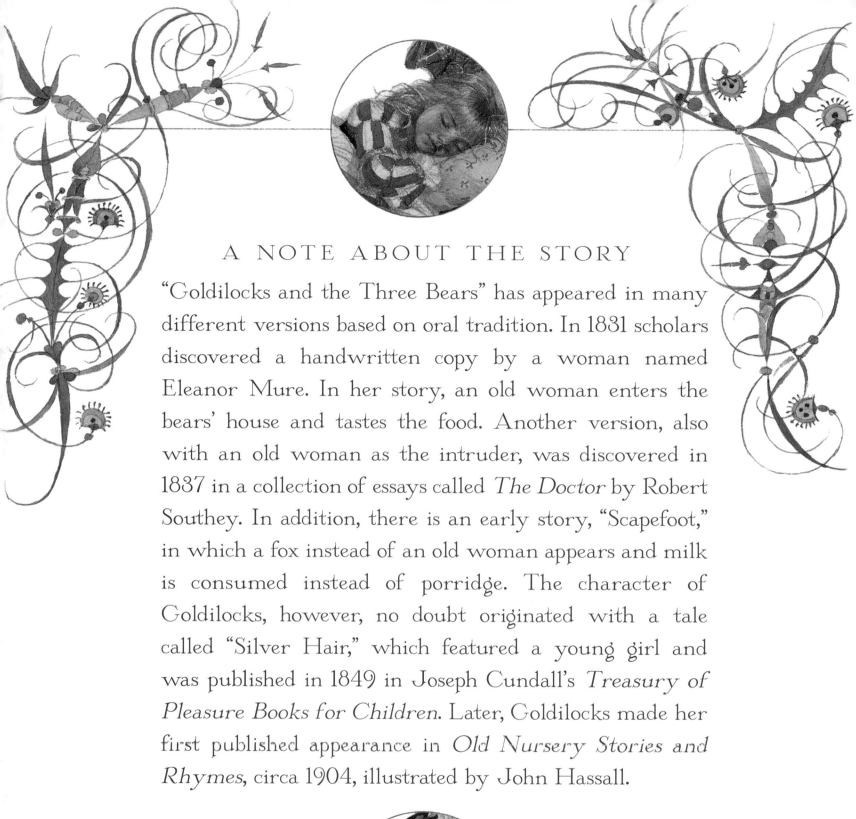

A NOTE ABOUT THE STORY

"Goldilocks and the Three Bears" has appeared in many different versions based on oral tradition. In 1831 scholars discovered a handwritten copy by a woman named Eleanor Mure. In her story, an old woman enters the bears' house and tastes the food. Another version, also with an old woman as the intruder, was discovered in 1837 in a collection of essays called *The Doctor* by Robert Southey. In addition, there is an early story, "Scapefoot," in which a fox instead of an old woman appears and milk is consumed instead of porridge. The character of Goldilocks, however, no doubt originated with a tale called "Silver Hair," which featured a young girl and was published in 1849 in Joseph Cundall's *Treasury of Pleasure Books for Children*. Later, Goldilocks made her first published appearance in *Old Nursery Stories and Rhymes*, circa 1904, illustrated by John Hassall.

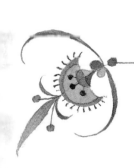
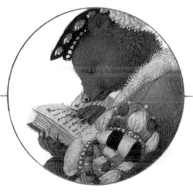

A NOTE ABOUT THE ARTIST

Gennady Spirin was born near Moscow and classically educated at the Moscow Art School at the Academy of Art and at the Moscow Stroganov Institute. He has received five gold medals from the Society of Illustrators in New York City, the Golden Apple at the Bratislava International Biennial, and first prize at both the Bologna and Barcelona international book fairs. His work has appeared four separate times on the annual *New York Times* Ten Best Illustrated Books of the Year list.

Mr. Spirin, now a U.S. citizen, lives in Princeton, New Jersey, with his wife and three sons.